TALKING IT THROUGH

Come and Tell Me

Helen Hollick

Illustrated by Lynda Knott

Happy Cat Books

Jenny McCann lives in the middle of a busy town. Because there are lots of houses and no gardens Jenny usually plays with her friends in the playground.

Mrs McCann keeps an eye on Jenny from the house. Jenny waves whenever she sees her mum.

One hot afternoon Jenny was playing with her friend
Darren. They took turns at pushing each other on the
swing, but it was hot work.

"My mum has some ice cream in the freezer," said
Darren. "Shall we go and ask her for some?"
"Oh, yes please!" said Jenny.
So they ran off to where Darren lived.

When Mrs McCann looked out of the window, she couldn't see Jenny anywhere. She hurried across to the playground and asked the other children if they knew where Jenny was. She was very worried.

Just at that moment, Jenny and Darren came round the corner, licking their ice creams. "Where have you been?" scolded Mrs McCann. "You're a naughty girl to disappear like that!"

Jenny was upset and began to cry.
Why was Mum so angry?

Back indoors, Mrs McCann gave Jenny a big hug.
"I'm not really angry," she said, "but sometimes worrying
makes you say and feel things you don't mean."

"I was only at Darren's house," sniffed Jenny.
"But I didn't know that, did I?" Mum answered.
"Listen," she explained, as she sat down on the floor
next to Jenny.

"There are lots of people in the world. Most of them are good, kind people but there are a few who are bad and wicked. It is not always easy to tell the good people from the bad people. When I couldn't see you in the playground, I thought perhaps a bad person had taken you away."

"Darren has been told
never to talk to a stranger,"
replied Jenny.

"Do you know who a stranger is?" Mum asked.
Jenny answered immediately. "Yes. A stranger is
someone I don't know. Someone I've never met before."
"That's right," said Mum, "but not all strangers are bad
people."

Mum said, " Sometimes you have to talk to someone you don't know. You might need to ask a stranger for help." She added, "Do you remember when you fell off your bike?"

Yes, Jenny did remember! She had cut her knee badly, and a stranger, a man she had never seen before, had asked if she was alright.

The man asked if anyone could get her mum.
Darren knew that it was safer for friends to stay
together - but Jenny had lots of other friends with her,
so he and another boy ran off to Jenny's house.

The cut had hurt a lot, but felt much better when mum
had cleaned it and put a big pink plaster over it.

"And I had to ask for help when I got lost in the supermarket," added Jenny, remembering how frightened she had felt when she couldn't find her mum.

"Can you remember what you did?" Mum asked her. "Yes," Jenny answered, "I went to the place where you pay, and told the lady that I was lost. She got someone to call out your name over the loudspeakers."

"But!" said Mum very sternly, "you must remember that you must not *go* anywhere with *anyone* - whether it is a man or a lady, a stranger or someone you know. And you mustn't get into someone's car without first asking me, Dad, or your teacher or whoever is looking after you."

"The best and most important thing to do," Mum added "is always come and tell me where you want to go, even if it is only to Darren's. Come and tell me, or Dad or Aunt Rashida next door. As long as you tell one of us, we will know where you are and that you are safe."

dear mum
Aunty Rashida
nows were
I am !
lov Jenny x+

Jenny suddenly looked very thoughtful. "When I was at school yesterday," she said, "I was playing near the gate with Amina. A car stopped and the lady asked if we knew where Anthony Road was."

"And what did you do?" asked Mum, curiously.
"We ran to get a dinner lady," Jenny answered.
Mum smiled and made a "good" sign with her thumb,
"Well done!"
"I think that lady should have asked a grown-up," said Jenny very wisely.
"Yes," Mum replied, nodding her head, "she should."

Jenny thought about what Mum had been saying. Then she asked, "So how can you tell a bad person from a good person?"

"Well," Mum said, "a good person would not mind if you came to tell me where you wanted to go."

"So," said Jenny thinking carefully, "if someone *didn't* want me to come and tell you first, that person might be bad?"

Mum was very pleased. She nodded and smiled.

"Yes, that's right," she said.

Some days later, Jenny was sitting in the playground. A man walked by with his dog. He stopped.

"Hello, are you on your own?" he asked.

"I'm waiting for my friend Darren," replied Jenny. "I like your dog."

"Her name is Bess," said the man. "She has some puppies at home, would you like to come and see them?"

"Yes please!" said Jenny eagerly - then she remembered what Mum had said. "I must tell my mum where I am going."
"Oh, there's no need for that!" The man said with a big smile. "I'm sure your mum won't mind!"

Jenny wanted to go with him. He seemed such a kind and friendly man. "I only live round the corner," he added.

"No!" insisted Jenny. "I *must* tell Mum first. I won't be long!"

Jenny ran home to tell her mum about the man and his dog.
"Good girl!" said Mum, "you are quite right to come and
tell me and ask if you can go and see the puppies."
"He looked kind, and he said there wasn't
any need to come and tell you," Jenny
explained, "but I remembered what
you told me."
"I'm so glad you did!" said Mum
proudly as she gave Jenny a great
big hug.
"There are some puppies in the
pet shop," Mum added, "Shall
we go and see them instead?"